# OFFED IN OREGON

RAMBLING RV COZY MYSTERIES, BOOK 4

PATTI BENNING

D1523227

SUMMER PRESCOTT BOOKS PUBLISHING

**Copyright 2022 Summer Prescott Books**

All Rights Reserved. No part of this publication nor any of the information herein may be quoted from, nor reproduced, in any form, including but not limited to: printing, scanning, photocopying, or any other printed, digital, or audio formats, without prior express written consent of the copyright holder.

**This book is a work of fiction. Any similarities to persons, living or dead, places of business, or situations past or present, is completely unintentional.

# CHAPTER ONE

It was late morning, but fog still clung to the mossy trees. Born and raised in Michigan, Tulia Blake was no stranger to forests, but Oregon's temperate rain forest might have been on a different planet entirely. She'd already been hiking for an hour, and even with the clinging humidity in the air, she felt no urge to turn around yet. It had been three months since she left home, and she'd seen a good portion of the country by now, but she thought this old forest with its tall evergreen trees, the countless ferns, and the sound of a waterfall ahead might be her favorite spot yet.

On her shoulder, her African grey parrot, Cicero, let out an ear-piercing whistle. She didn't even flinch at the sound; he had been her companion her entire life, and she was no stranger to the array of strange noises he liked to make.

Reaching up to let him step onto her hand, she took him down from her shoulder. He was wearing a specially made avian harness with an elastic leash, which was clipped to her belt buckle with a carabiner. He'd gotten used to their hikes and walks in nature areas, and while he had been content to ride on her shoulder for the morning so far, he was ready to spread his wings.

"Okay, buddy," she said, her voice sounding unnatural in the quiet stillness of the forest. She'd gotten there early and hadn't seen any other hikers so far.

Carefully, she placed her parrot on top of a waist-high, moss-covered rock. He tilted his head to one side, eyeing it as he paced around on top, then looked back up at her, his wings quivering.

"Let's do what we've been practicing. Come—"

She broke off as he launched himself off the rock at her, his wings beating the air as he flew toward her face. She raised her hand just in time for him to swing his legs forward and grip her fingers. He gave an excited two-tone whistle, and she grinned.

"Great! You're getting so much better at this, Cicero. Let's try from a little farther away, okay?"

While Cicero's wings had never been clipped, he had never been a big flier either. She wanted to change that; at the beginning of her trip, he'd gotten out of her RV, and she had barely gotten him back. She also wanted him to have the chance to get exercise; he was thirty years old, and while African grey parrots could live to fifty or even longer, a good diet and plenty of exercise was essential. Cicero was very much a perch potato unless she got him up and moving—or, he had been. In the past few days, something seemed to have clicked in his mind, and he had fully realized what his wings were for.

Now, he flew to her almost every chance he got. She wanted to get him a longer leash—right now, he was limited to flights of about five feet outside, and the length of her RV indoors.

After practicing a few more flights, setting him on makeshift perches of different heights, he was breathing heavily, and she set him back on her shoulder. "Perch potato indeed. We'll get you flying fit in no time."

She resumed walking in silence, closing her eyes and taking a deep breath of the natural smells of dirt and wet wood. After leaving Montana, she had driven through the narrow tip of Idaho and the corner of Washington, just so she could say she'd been there, before making her way to Oregon. She was on her way toward the coast, where she wanted to stop by the Tillamook Creamery and go to the coast, and after that, see if she could find a tour of a vineyard somewhere between here and California.

Today, though, was purely one of relaxation. She and Cicero had spent way too much time in her RV over the last couple of days, and now they were taking the time to stretch their legs—or wings—and do some exploring. She'd left Montana behind quickly—maybe too quickly. She had been fleeing a serial killer and the memories of a man she had failed to save. Even though the killer was behind bars now, her experience in the state had been soured. She had wanted to get as far away as she could as quickly as possible, but now, she regretted it. She wished she'd spent more time in Idaho, or that she'd camped in Washington. She was tempted to detour out of her way just to see the movie-famous small town of Forks, but by the time she thought of it, she'd already been in Oregon.

There was no rush. If she decided she wanted to

go back and visit the states she hadn't done much in other than drive through, she could. It was so strange —even after nearly half a year, she still hadn't gotten used to the fact that her life was forever changed thanks to the impulse buy of a single lottery ticket. No more waitressing long hours just to make ends meet. No more living in a too small, too expensive apartment. No more daydreaming about the life she wanted; now, she could live it.

The path changed course, heading uphill, and she slowed her pace. While she had gone on more hikes and nature walks in the past few months than she had in the years beforehand, she still wasn't exactly in the greatest shape. She spent a lot of time behind the wheel of her RV and gave in to the temptation of eating snack foods and takeout from restaurants a bit too often. By the time she reached the top of the hill, she was breathing heavily, and shot a mock glare at Cicero's gray form on her shoulder. "I wouldn't be out of breath if I didn't have to lug you around, you know. This is all your fault."

He ran his beak through a section of her hair, and she winced as he pulled just a bit too hard on one of the strands. Raising her hand to scratch his head fondly, she took a deep breath and gazed forward at the trail. Maybe she should start heading back soon. It was getting toward noon, and she hadn't eaten since eight that morning. While she had a bottle of water with her, she hadn't brought any snacks, and she was beginning to feel hungry.

"Maybe I'll just go another mile or—" She broke off mid-sentence at the chilling sound of a scream piercing the air. It was only after the sound faded that she realized how quiet it was around her. Too quiet. She'd been enjoying the silence, but only now realized that she wasn't hearing any birds or even insects. Goosebumps rose on her arms, and she took half a step back toward the way she'd come.

But the scream stayed with her, even though it hadn't repeated. What if another hiker had gotten hurt? She might be the only one around who could help them.

She waited a few seconds longer, but the scream didn't come again. It had seemed to come from the direction she was already going in, so she double-checked that her pepper spray was easy to reach, took a bracing breath, and kept on walking.

She would go another mile or two and see if she could find whoever had screamed. If not, she would call it a day and head back to the parking lot, where she had left her car. If she did find someone, she would offer what help she could. If someone was hurt out here, she might be their only chance for a rescue until friends or family realized they were missing, which could be hours or even days down the line. She would never be able to live with herself if she didn't at least try.

## CHAPTER TWO

The clouds were beginning to clear, and with the added sunlight, the fog was burning away. The air was still humid, though, and air-conditioning was sounding more and more inviting, but she wasn't ready to give up yet. She'd been walking for about ten minutes and hadn't heard or seen any signs of whoever it was who had screamed, but she wanted to go just a bit further. The trail curved a little bit ahead, and she wanted to see what was past that.

When she reached the curve in the trail, she realized it wasn't just a curve—the trail split off in a Y. The path to the right was obviously the more traveled one, with a bench and a waterproof map nailed to a post. The one that went to the left looked almost like a game trail, but she could see boot prints in the wet soil. Someone had gone down there recently. Pausing at the crossroads, she bit her lip as she considered her choices. Finally, she decided to go to the left. If someone had gotten injured, it was probably more likely to have happened on a less well-groomed trail.

The path went downhill, and she let her feet carry her as she looked around. It wasn't until she smelled a thick, musky smell in the air that she came to a slow stop, the fine hairs at the back of her neck prickling. Had the scream been the call of some sort of animal? She had read up on Oregon's wildlife, and knew it had quite a few large animals, including deer, elk, cougar, and beaver. Born and raised in Michigan, she was no stranger to deer and knew they didn't make a sound anything close to the scream she'd heard, and she doubted beavers made that sort of noise either, but could it have been a cougar or an elk she'd heard? Was she walking right towards an angry or injured wild animal?

She wavered but continued on despite her misgivings. The scent only grew stronger as she continued down the trail, and before long, she saw a clearing through the trees with a bright blue tent in it. A campsite.

"Hello?" she called out as she continued walking down the trail, approaching the turnoff for the campsite. There was no response. She wondered if this was where the scream had come from. She hoped no one was seriously injured. Maybe they'd stepped out of their tent and seen whatever animal left this strong, unpleasant, musky smell, and had screamed because they were frightened.

She tried calling out again. "Is anyone there? I heard someone scream. Do you need help?"

She reached the turnoff for the campsite, which was a short muddy trail, but paused before she stepped onto it. There was a footprint in the mud. Not a shoeprint; it was barefoot, and it didn't look human. For one thing, it was three times the size of her own foot.

"No way," she murmured. She wasn't superstitious, but she'd had fun listening to podcasts about Bigfoot as she'd driven toward the West Coast. Most of what she'd heard had been laughably fake, but some of the more plausible stories came back to her now.

The footprint she was looking at in the mud couldn't belong to a human, unless he was the largest and heaviest human who had ever existed. Suddenly, the heavy, musky scent in the air seemed even more ominous, and she looked into the deep forest around her. Something in a bush just off the trail caught her attention, and carefully avoiding the big footprint, she approached it. It was a tuft of thick, brown hair—no, fur. She touched it and pulled her hand back. It felt rough and almost greasy. There was another big footprint on the ground in front of her, and she realized they were leading directly toward the tent. A tent which, from this angle, she could see was half-collapsed.

"No freaking way."

She hurried into the clearing, Cicero gripping her shoulder tightly with his claws, and she was careful not to step on any of the mysterious prints in the mud. She was only a few feet away from the tent when she saw the first droplets of blood, splattered across the blue fabric of the tent in dark red which had looked like black mud from a distance. She stumbled to a stop, Cicero nearly losing his balance on her shoulder. He smacked her in the head with a wing as he fluttered to keep from falling, but she didn't even blink. She was staring at the tent. At the splatter of blood on the tent, and at the too-still pair of booted feet sticking out from behind it.

Feeling almost faint from how quickly her heart was beating, she walked around the tent and had to press her hands to her mouth when she saw what was behind it. He was a man, she could tell that much, but he had died from a horrible head wound. In the mud around him were more of the large prints, and one of his hands was clutching a handful of the dirty, brown fur.

"Oh, my goodness," she breathed. She took a hesitant step closer, then paused. There was nothing she could do to help. And … whoever had screamed, it hadn't been him. It had sounded like a woman.

Realizing that someone else might be around, she started looking for clues and found more prints—boot prints this time—leading into the forest opposite the tent. They looked fresh, or at least, that was her guess since she wasn't an expert tracker.

She hesitated only a second before following them. She didn't want to be in the clearing any longer than she had to in case who or whatever had killed the man came back. And this woman might be injured, she might need Tulia's help. Besides, the fact that there were no Bigfoot tracks in the mud in this direction was reassuring. Not that she believed it was Bigfoot. That was impossible … right?

She waited until she was a good distance away from the clearing before she called out again. Cicero punctuated her words with a sharp whistle. She'd been following the sporadic boot prints through the wet soil, but wasn't sure she was on the right path anymore. The ground was covered in moss, ferns, and decaying logs, and it was difficult to pick out the occasional track.

"Hello? Is anyone out here?"

There was a faint noise to her left. She turned and saw a flash of pink, which resolved itself into a woman hiding behind a tree. The woman must have seen her looking, because she stepped out from behind it. There were dark splatters on the front of her coat that could have been mud or blood.

"H-hello?"

"Are you okay?" Tulia asked. "Did you scream earlier?"

The woman nodded, rubbing at her eyes. It looked as if she'd been crying. "It—it attacked him. Mason. He needs help. P-please, I need to call an ambulance. Do you have a phone? Is that a bird on your shoulder?"

The woman seemed utterly confused by Cicero's presence. "He's my pet," she explained quickly. "Are you talking about the man back at the tent? Is he Mason?"

The woman nodded. Tulia bit her lip, not sure what to say. The man was long past any help. "I'm sorry," she said instead. "Are you hurt? Do you need my help? My car is in the parking lot, and if you need to go to the hospital, I can drive you."

"I twisted my ankle," the woman said. "I don't know which way to go, and I keep having to stop because my ankle hurts. I thought it was chasing me, and I wasn't paying attention to where I was going."

"Why don't you sit down? Let me see if I can find you a stick or something you can use to make it easier to walk."

It was a few minutes before she spotted a promising branch and picked it up from the ground, brushing it off before bringing it over to the woman, who took it gratefully. She looked shaken, and Tulia could see that her ankle was swelling and turning purple already. She couldn't blame the woman for being terrified after what she had seen… Whatever that had been.

"My name is Tulia," she offered. "I'll help you get to help, okay?"

"Melody," the woman said. "And my boyfriend is Mason. Did you see him? It is—is he…?"

"I don't think he made it," Tulia admitted gently. Melody's body was racked with a sob, and Tulia put a hand on her shoulder, not sure what to do. She turned, intending to start finding a path for them back toward the main trail, then hesitated. She wasn't sure which direction she had come from.

"Do you know which direction you came from?" she asked the woman.

Melody sniffed, wiping her face and shaking her head. She hesitated, then said, "You don't know where we are either, do you?"

"I don't," Tulia admitted. "But I know I went uphill at one point, so let's just keep heading downhill. That should lead us somewhere eventually, right?"

Melody nodded hesitantly, wiping at her eyes again. Tulia helped her up and using the walking stick, the other woman began to walk.

It was slow going. They walked for a long time—it must have been close to two hours, and Tulia was beginning to wonder if they would ever find the trail.

She should have thought twice before leaving it, but she hadn't even considered the dangers of getting lost out here. She'd been too freaked out by what she found in the clearing, and then had been concerned about the person whose footsteps she was following. But now, she was concerned about both of them. What would they do if they couldn't make their way back to the trail? She knew that the advice was to stay where you were if you got lost in the forest, but no one knew she was even out here. No one would come looking for her here, and Melody didn't seem to be in any condition to wait, anyway. Besides, who or whatever had killed Mason was still out here.

"We'll be out soon," she said when Melody began to lag behind, trying to be encouraging. "Do you have family nearby? We can call them first thing."

"No," she sniffed. "I have no one, now that Mason is … is hurt."

Tulia bit her lip, not sure what to say. She was on the verge of asking Melody to sit on a log and wait while she took off on her own to look for the trail when Melody grabbed her arm.

"Do you hear that?"

"What?" Tulia asked, her pulse ratcheting up another notch.

"Voices."

They both fell silent, and after a moment, Tulia heard the sound of multiple voices talking in the distance. The two of them turned toward the sound and began picking their way through the forest toward it. Before long, Tulia saw a gap in the trees, then the bright red of someone's clothing. She increased her pace, only pausing when Melody began to stumble again. Within seconds, they burst out onto the trail. She didn't remember which direction the parking lot was in, but there were trail signs and maps interspersed along the hiking paths. She felt a rush of relief. Worst case scenario now, she would just follow the trail until she found a map and could see where they were.

They had come out of the trees behind a group of people, but they had been loud enough that the hikers turned around. One of the men called out, "Whoa, are you two okay?" His companions all turned as well and began reversing down the trail heading back toward them.

"She's injured," Tulia said, helping Melody over to a fallen tree along the path so she could sit down again. "We're trying to get back to the parking lot so I can take her to the hospital."

"What happened?" the man who had already spoken asked.

"It—it attacked him," Melody said, propping her foot up. Her ankle looked even worse, and Tulia wondered if they should try to elevate it or something. "It—it killed Mason."

"What did?" the man asked, crouching down in front of her. Tulia looked over the group; there were three of them in total, two men and a woman. Each of them was carrying some sort of equipment—it looked like cameras, mostly, and other recording equipment.

They had rugged hiking packs stuffed to the brim and were all wearing waterproof boots and windbreakers.

Melody glanced at Tulia before focusing on the man. "Bigfoot," she said, taking a deep breath. "Bigfoot attacked us. I saw it with my own eyes."

# CHAPTER THREE

The group exploded into conversation at Melody's statement. To Tulia's surprise, one of the men, the one in a green windbreaker with a pair of thick-rimmed glasses, let out a whoop. The woman clasped her hands to her face, but the expression looked like one of excitement rather than horror, and the man who had been talking just raised a skeptical eyebrow.

"Someone died," Tulia snapped. "And Melody's hurt. If you're not going to help us, then get out of our way so I can keep helping her back toward the parking lot."

That sobered the group up quickly, though she could still see the eagerness in the eyes of two of the members. The one who looked skeptical came forward and helped Melody up, letting her lean on him. He had long brown hair and light, watery-blue eyes, which stared at Cicero for a moment before focusing on her. "I'm sorry," he said. "We're cryptid hunters. We came out here looking for Bigfoot, or, those two did. I came out here so I could make fun of them while they look for something that doesn't exist. I'm Emmerson Quinn. I'll help the two of you back to the parking lot."

"Where was the Bigfoot attack?" the man in the green windbreaker asked. The woman elbowed him.

"Read the room, Norman. We'll help them back to the parking lot, and once an ambulance is on the way, maybe we can get the information from them. Look at her, she's really hurt. And … is someone really dead?"

Melody and Emmerson began to make their way down the trail, and Tulia followed slowly behind them, Norman and the woman falling into step beside her. Tulia nodded, falling back a little so she could talk quietly without Melody hearing. She didn't think the other woman needed to deal with anything else right now.

"I saw his body myself. I was hiking when I heard a scream. A little ways down the trail, I came to their camp. The guy she was with—something killed him. It was really bad. She'd already run off into the woods, and I was lucky to even find her; we both got lost after that."

"Do you think you'd be able to find the campsite again?" the woman asked. "For thc police, of course."

Tulia raised an eyebrow. The woman still seemed a bit too eager, but she answered honestly. "Yeah, I should be able to. It was just off the trail. If you follow it for long enough I'm sure you'd come across it. I don't think anyone should go there until the police have a chance to look things over, though."

"Of course, if someone is really dead, that's more important than finding proof of Bigfoot." The woman held out her hand as they walked, and Tulia shook it. "I'm Thea Higgins. And this jerk is Norman Crane."

"Hey, I'm not a jerk," Norman said from Tulia's other side. "I was just excited. I've been looking for proof like this my whole life. Of course, it's horrible that someone was killed and someone else was hurt, but can you imagine how famous we would be if this is real? This might be the proof we need. People will actually listen to us now."

"Norman, our only eyewitness is a traumatized woman who saw her friend die and can barely walk," Thea hissed back. "No offense to her, but she's not exactly the most reliable witness."

"If it really was a Bigfoot attack, there will be

evidence in the area," Norman said. He turned to Tulia eagerly. "Did you see anything? Footprints, maybe?"

She hesitated. Despite everything she'd seen, she wasn't convinced the culprit was actually Bigfoot. Maybe it was a bear? She'd have to look at bear prints online once she got out of this forest.

She sighed and admitted, "It definitely smelled like some sort of animal had been there, and I saw a few clumps of fur. I did see footprints in the muck, but I don't know what animal they belonged to. I'm no wildlife expert. I do think it was an animal attack, but I'm not about to say it was Bigfoot."

"Come on, this is Bigfoot country," Norman said, gesturing to the forest around them. "I can't believe it. The stroke of luck—"

Thea kicked him around Tulia's legs, and he jumped back, yelping, then shot Tulia and the other woman a chagrined look. "Sorry, sorry. I'll shut up now."

Silence fell over their group after that. Tulia wanted to know more about what they actually did in their hunt for cryptids, but indulging in her curiosity didn't feel right after what Melody had gone through. The going was slow, but it was mostly downhill, and before too long, maybe another forty-five minutes, she saw the open expanse of the parking lot through the trees. Melody let out a sob of relief.

"Do you want me to bring your car around?" Tulia asked. "We will probably have to wait here for the police, but I'm sure you'll be more comfortable if you can sit down."

"I left my keys at the campsite," Melody said. "I don't have anything, not even my purse."

Tulia hadn't thought of that. "I have an RV," she offered. "You'll probably be most comfortable in there. If you want to wait, I can bring it—"

"I can walk across the parking lot," Melody said. "Thanks."

It took them another few minutes to walk the rest of the way to the parking lot and to cross it to where her RV was parked. She unlocked the door and stepped inside, reaching down to help Melody up the steps. She guided the woman over to the couch and went over to Cicero's cage to put him inside, taking his harness off. The screen door fell shut as the last of the small group stepped inside. They looked around, and Norman let out a low whistle.

"Now, this is what we need. We might actually be able to afford something like this after—"

"Dude, would you shut up?" Emmerson asked, turning on his companion. "Just drop the Bigfoot talk, all right? This is serious. No one wants to hear your unfounded theories right now."

"Well, sorry if I'm just a little bit excited to actually have a real Bigfoot attack right at our fingertips. This is what we were looking for, am I wrong? Am I supposed to just ignore it? A stroke of luck like this is not going to fall into our laps again."

"It's not luck," Emmerson snapped. "Someone died, either from an animal attack or the actions of another person, and you can't stop talking about an imaginary ape."

"I knew I shouldn't have let you come along," Norman replied.

"Would the both of you be quiet?" Thea snapped. "We've got more important things to focus on right now. Do any of you have a phone that has service out here? We should call the police and an ambulance for Melody."

"Right," Tulia said. Melody was sitting on the couch lengthwise, her foot propped up on the far armrest. She didn't look like she was paying attention to the conversation; she seemed lost in her shock and pain. Tulia took her phone out of her pocket and spotted a single, measly bar of service. It would have to do. Dialing 911, she raised the phone to her ear.

It took the police nearly an hour to arrive. During

that time, she had to sit through two more arguments between the cryptid hunters and a very awkward and sad ten-minute stretch where Melody started crying and couldn't stop. She offered everyone water and snacks, and while they accepted the former, everyone turned down the latter. Norman looked like he was going to accept, but Thea kicked him again, and he shut up, going to sit sullenly in a chair.

Conversation started and stopped in spurts; they asked her about her RV and gave her advice for a local campground with RV hookups when she admitted she didn't know where to camp tonight, and she asked a few questions about what they did, but fell silent when Melody started sniffling again.

When the police arrived, it was with a secondary team who were dressed in raincoats and hiking gear. A pair of uniformed officers came to the RV and began questioning Melody. Tulia gave the other team directions to the campsite as best she could. Thankfully, they didn't need her to go with them, because she wasn't sure she could handle another long hike just then.

Tulia told the story again when it was her turn to be questioned, telling the officers everything she could remember. Then, it was a waiting game. It took the team an hour and a half to locate the campsite, and when they radioed back, the officer who spoke into the radio returned to the RV with a concerned look on his face.

"We found the scene," he began. "We may need to ask some of you to come in for further questioning. Do you plan on staying in the area for the next few days?"

"I can stick around for a while," Tulia said.

"We're definitely sticking around," Norman said, speaking for his group.

The officer nodded. "Good. I'll give you all my number. I'm not going to ask you not to leave the area, but if you do, I would appreciate a heads-up. None of you are suspects at this point, but it's possible you've seen or heard something that might help us out."

"What about Melody?" she asked, looking over to where the woman was being loaded up into an ambulance. "Will she be okay?"

"Her ankle is her only serious injury," the officer said. "She'll be all right. She's lucky you found her when you did. People die of exposure out here sometimes. Getting lost is no joke."

Tulia's gaze lingered on Melody, watching as the paramedics shut the ambulance doors and pulled out of the parking lot.

# CHAPTER FOUR

Once the police were done questioning her, Tulia parted ways with the others. Even though the officers had stressed that the campsite was currently a crime scene, she had the feeling they were going to try to sneak back to it at some point soon, and she didn't want to be involved with any of it.

Despite what she'd seen at the campsite, she couldn't believe that Bigfoot had really attacked Melody and Mason. It was just too absurd. She just hoped that the cryptid hunting team didn't do anything to mess up Melody's case. Were the police treating it as an animal attack, she wondered, or a homicide?

The RV park Emmerson had suggested to her was a basic one; not much more than a place for people to park and hook up to water and sewage, but it wasn't very busy, and the view was phenomenal, with tall trees all around. She was one of only three RVs there, and the campground had space for ten times that number.

She still loved the natural landscape of Oregon, but some of the magic of her time here had vanished. Despite her certainty that there was no Bigfoot out there, *something* or some*one* had to be behind the attack, and she didn't feel safe going into the woods alone anymore.

She was too tired to get to it that evening, but the next morning, she updated her blog, mentioning that she had helped a woman out of the woods, promising to go into more detail later. She didn't want to say too much in case it somehow affected the ongoing case, so she filled most of her post with photos of her and Cicero enjoying the hike.

Then, she went through and checked the new comments on her last post. She responded to the nice ones, ignored the occasional weird or mean comment, and kept a sharp eye out for comments that might have been left by her ex, Luis. While she had blocked anonymous comments, he had taken to creating accounts just so he could harass her on her blog. He had been bothering her almost every day since he found out about her lottery winnings, and it was just getting worse.

She wished he would just let it go. The only reason he wasn't out here with her right now was because he had cheated on her. *She* wasn't the one who had thrown their relationship away, but he still seemed to blame her for leaving him. He had even gone so far as to hire a private investigator to track her down.

As if thinking about him had summoned him, her phone rang with another unknown Michigan number. She sent it to voicemail with a groan. Why couldn't he just leave her be?

Frustrated, she logged out of her blogging account and stretched, looking out the window. It was another gray, overcast day. She wasn't sure what she wanted to do. She had spent a fair amount of time out in nature these past couple of weeks; maybe it was time to head into town and do some exploring there. She wished she'd gotten Melody's number, though there hadn't been an appropriate time to ask. She really wanted an update on the case.

If she was going into town anyway, maybe she could visit Melody at the hospital. The other woman had said she didn't have any local relatives or friends. She might appreciate seeing a friendly face, and then

Tulia could assuage her own curiosity. She just wanted to know if the police had found the culprit yet. She was willing to bet her entire lottery winnings that it wasn't really Bigfoot, but that didn't mean who or whatever had attacked the camp wasn't dangerous and violent.

She left Cicero in the RV with the temperature control running and the doors locked and took her sedan into town, enjoying the ease of driving a normally sized vehicle instead of the behemoth she spent most of her time in. She had a few things she wanted to pick up at the grocery store, but she could leave that for last. Her first stop was to a small coffee shop where she got a blueberry flavored latte and a red velvet cupcake that looked too good to turn down. By the time she reached the hospital, the caffeine and sugar was getting to her, and she felt jittery.

Inside, she made her way up to the front desk and then realized she only knew Melody's first name. She didn't know if they would let her in with just that, but she might as well try; she was already here, after all.

The woman looked skeptical, but when she explained that she'd found Melody lost in the woods yesterday and wanted to see how she was doing, recognition seemed to dawn in her eyes. It was a small hospital, and she supposed people talked about cases as interesting as Melody's.

"She's accepting visitors. She's up on the third floor, in room 308. I'll get you a pass. Visiting hours end at eight in the evening."

"Thanks," Tulia said, accepting the name tag, which she stuck on herself. It was just before eleven in the morning now; she doubted visiting hours would be an issue.

She took the elevator up to the third floor and followed the signs to room 308. The door was already propped open, and she stepped forward, about to knock on the doorframe, when she heard voices coming from inside.

Curious and hoping she wasn't interrupting if one of Melody's family members had flown out to visit her, she peeked in. All three cryptid hunters were gathered around Melody's bed.

Tulia felt a surge of irritation; could they not let this go? Did they really, truly believe Bigfoot had killed Melody's friend?

She rapped on the doorframe, sharper than she'd intended, and everyone turned to look at her. Forcing a smile to her face, she stepped into the room. "Hi, Melody," she said. "Sorry to just drop in. I wanted to see how you were doing."

Melody gave her a weak smile and glanced down at her ankle, which was in a sturdy looking plastic boot. "Well, probably better than I would be doing if you hadn't found me," she said. "Thanks for that. Sorry if I didn't say it yesterday."

"Hey, don't worry about it," Tulia said, moving closer to the bed. Emmerson stepped aside so she could take his spot. "You have a lot going on. Is your ankle going to be okay?"

"It's broken, so I've got quite a few weeks in this cast, and then I'll have physical therapy, but it should heal up pretty well." Her voice was subdued, without much inflection. She gave a small shrug. "Other than that, I've just got some scrapes and bruises."

"Have you heard anything from the police?"

The other woman shook her head. "Nothing. One of the ones in uniform said she'd stop by to talk to me today, but I haven't seen her yet."

"We were just on our way out," Emmerson said to Tulia. "We wanted to stop and see how Melody was doing—and apologize for our behavior yesterday."

Norman looked like his friends had given him a serious talking to. He was a lot more subdued than he had been, and he gave Tulia an embarrassed smile.

"Yeah. I really am sorry. I see now that the way I acted was completely inappropriate. I know it's not a good excuse, but I've spent my whole life hoping to find Bigfoot or some other cryptid. People always mocked me for it, even my own family. I just… I lost sight of things when she said it was a Bigfoot attack."

"I've forgiven him," Melody said firmly when she saw Tulia about to object. "If I'm being honest, I barely even remember anything he said yesterday. I was too out of it. Everything is a blur. I'm glad they're here because I know the police are on the wrong track. No person did that to my Mason. It was Bigfoot. I saw him. I was just feet away from him." She held Tulia's eyes. "I'm not crazy, and I'm not lying. I know what I saw. Do you believe me?"

Tulia hesitated. "I'm sure you saw something. I'm sorry, I know this isn't what you want to hear, but I just don't think I can believe in something like Bigfoot. I don't think you're lying, but there has to be another explanation for it."

Melody pressed her lips together but gave a resigned nod. "I know how crazy I sound, but I want Mason to get justice. That's why I'm glad they're here helping me. They're going to find Bigfoot for me, and then the world will know what really happened to the man I loved."

Before Tulia could say anything else, a nurse knocked sharply on the doorframe and came bustling into the room. Thea, who had been sitting in the chair next Melody's bed, stood up. "Well, I think we're going to head out now. We'll come visit again soon. Don't give up, all right?"

"Thanks," Melody said, fighting back a yawn as the nurse checked her IV. "I actually think I'm going to take a nap. The hospital's going to release me later today, but I'm exhausted right now."

"I'll head out too," Tulia said. She squeezed Melody's hand. "I'll leave you my number, all right? If you need anything, just call me. I'm staying at Bigleaf RV Park, which is only about twenty minutes from here."

Melody sleepily gestured to a notepad and pen beside her bed. Tulia scribbled down her number, then said a final goodbye and stepped out of the room where the cryptid team was waiting. She was about to say her goodbyes to them when Emmerson cleared his throat.

"Hey, we were talking. We're all going to go get brunch. Do you want to join us? You're more than welcome to. I think you and I have similar opinions on what happened, so maybe we'll be able to convince these two crazies that they're wrong." He gestured to his friends, who looked more amused than insulted.

She hesitated, but company for brunch sounded nice. While she wasn't sure she was a huge fan of Norman, and she still didn't know what she thought of Thea. Emmerson seemed all right, and Norman *had* apologized for his behavior. And with Emmerson there, at least she wouldn't be the only one who thought the whole Bigfoot thing was far-fetched.

"Sure," she decided. "I'll tag along. Where are we going?"

They told her the name of a restaurant, which she typed into her phone's GPS, and they walked out of the hospital together. Tulia would eat her purse before she became a cryptid hunter, but it was nice, for now, to feel like she was part of a team.

# CHAPTER FIVE

They found a small diner not far from the hospital. The first thing that greeted Tulia when she stepped through the door was a chalkboard sign proclaiming that the diner had the best blueberry pie in the city. The second was a cheery middle-aged waitress who waved them in and told them they could sit wherever they wanted. Norman took the lead, heading toward a booth on the quieter side of the room, away from the rambunctious family in the corner.

After taking their drink order, which was coffee and water all around, the waitress left them with their menus. Tulia looked at hers, but was only half paying attention to it. Emmerson sat beside her, with Thea and Norman across from them. The three were talking like old friends, which she supposed they were. And of course, the topic was Bigfoot.

"It will probably take us a couple of hours even once we get out there," Thea was saying. It had the feel of the conversation that had been continued from earlier. "We won't want to go too late in the day. It would be best to be out of there before dark, especially if there really is a cryptid out there."

"The later we go the better," Norman said, his voice tinged with annoyance. "We don't want the cops walking in on us. If we get up there at, say, seven, it's probably later than the police would come, and it still gives us an hour or so of daylight. Plus, we have our headlights and flashlights. We'll be fine even after dark."

"The park closes at nine," Emmerson said. "The only way we'd be able to do that is if only two of us go and the other person drives the truck away so we don't get ticketed. The person who stays behind could pick you up at the gates when you make it back down from the trails."

"And you'll be the one who stays back?" Norman asked. He scoffed. "Of course. You're afraid to see any evidence that might change your mind."

Emmerson bristled, but before the conversation could devolve into an argument, Tulia put her menu down. "Are you guys talking about going back to the scene of the murder?"

"Murder?" Norman turned toward her, one of his eyebrows arching. "It was a wild animal attack. Being killed by Bigfoot is like being killed by a … a moose, or something. While they are more intelligent than most animals, and some people have even reported observing tool use, they are still animals. I wouldn't call what happened to that man murder."

"Sorry, I misspoke," Tulia said, not trying to start anything. "I was just asking, because if you're going back to an active crime scene, you could end up derailing the police investigation."

"We'll just be looking for evidence that confirms our theory," Thea said. "The most we'll leave behind is footprints. The most we'll take will be pictures … and maybe some clumps of fur if we find any. We don't want to impede the police from their investigation at all. If they follow it to its logical conclusion, they'll realize it's Bigfoot too, and that's the whole point. We're here to prove to the world Bigfoot exists."

"They're here to prove to the world that an imaginary animal exists," Emmerson said. "I'm just tagging along because I like making fun of them and, for some unknown reason, we're friends, and doing stuff like this can be fun even if it's stupid."

"Look, I respect that you don't believe, but do you have to keep saying stuff like that?" Norman asked, irritated again. "It's one thing to be a skeptic, it's another to constantly rag on our beliefs."

"You take yourself too seriously," Emmerson said, rolling his eyes. "But fine, I'll keep my mouth shut for now."

He glanced at the menu again, and Tulia spotted the waitress coming over out of the corner of her eye, carrying a tray laden with coffee and water. She picked up her own menu and looked it over. She wasn't sure what she wanted. Finally, she settled on the blueberry pancakes with hashbrowns and bacon. It had been a while since she'd had good breakfast food, and while it wasn't exactly the healthiest choice, at least it had fruit in it.

"Emmerson," Thea said once the waitress had taken their orders. "I know you don't believe in Bigfoot. I didn't either at first, but after what we've seen, how can you keep denying it? There's something out there. Melody says she saw it with her own eyes. Are you calling her a liar? And what about Tulia? She doesn't believe either, but everything she described is in line with what we know about Bigfoot attacks."

"Melody is traumatized," Emmerson said. "I'm not calling her a liar, and whatever happened to her and that guy, Mason, was horrific, but I think it's very possible and even plausible that in her fear and terror, she built up whatever she saw in her mind into something more monstrous than it really was. Frankly, I don't think we should even be involving her in this investigation at all. Let the poor woman heal, both physically and mentally."

"She seemed pretty eager to help us out when we visited her," Norman said. "I think she wants the truth to come out."

"Why did you guys visit her, anyway?" Tulia asked, sipping her coffee. She added another creamer and then tried it again. This place might have the best blueberry pie in town, but it definitely needed to work on how it brewed its coffee.

"We wanted to go over what she saw when she was in a better state of mind, and we figured she'd be more with it today than she was yesterday," he said. "I know it probably sounds bad, but we were careful not to upset her. She's the one who started sharing details. She really wants to help us bring this to light. The world needs to know."

"I know I'm not part of your team, but I'm not sold on the idea of you guys investigating this yourselves. Regardless of whether you believe it was a Bigfoot attack or not, interfering in a police investigation is not a good idea. And for all we know, they have evidence that we don't. Heck, for all we know, Melody herself is a suspect. Statistically, most murder victims are killed by someone they're close to."

"So, what, you think she's saying it was a Bigfoot attack to throw us off the trail?" Norman asked. "If that was the case, wouldn't she choose something more believable? Most people are just as skeptical as you and Emmerson are."

"I don't know," Tulia said, raising her hands. "I'm just saying, maybe you shouldn't go back to an active crime scene?"

The waitress returned with the food before Norman could reply, and that sidetracked all of them. Tulia was glad. She hadn't known the man very long, and she was sure in other situations he was just fine, but she couldn't help being irritated by his attitude. He was acting like everyone else was stupid for not believing in a myth. She was all for respecting other people's beliefs, but this was just absurd.

She remembered the way she felt when she walked into the campsite with the heavy, musky animal smell and the footprints and clumps of fur, but pushed the feeling aside. Now, in the daylight, with the sun peeking through the clouds and coming in through the diner's window, it was easy to dismiss the possibility that Bigfoot was real.

"Oh, hey, Melody finally accepted my friend request," Thea said, looking down at her phone. "And, Norman, I hate to break it to you, but Tulia might actually have a point."

"What?" They spoke at the same time, and Norman shot her another glare as if it was her fault before turning back to his companion.

"So this Mason guy, he was her boyfriend, but it looks like they were having issues. Get this, a couple months ago, she posted 'I gave my heart to you and you broke it. I never thought you would betray me like this. How can you rebuild trust once it's shattered?'" Thea raised her eyebrows. "It's vague, but I'm guessing it was probably directed toward her boyfriend. From the comments underneath it, it sounds like he cheated on her, but she doesn't go into specifics. A little while later she posted something about second chances. It definitely sounds like they had their issues. What if she found out he cheated on her again? Maybe things got violent, and she tried to cover it up by faking a Bigfoot attack."

"Come on, that's a stretch," Norman said. "You really think that woman went to all the trouble to do that, then wandered off into the woods, broke her own ankle, and put her life at risk, instead of just pushing him off a cliff and saying he fell or something? You're supposed to be on my side with this. Don't tell me you're suddenly ditching me for the land of the skeptics."

"I'm not, I'm just saying we should consider all possibilities. This is why no one takes cryptid hunters seriously. They're too quick to jump on what they want the answer to be instead of just trying to find the truth."

"In this case, what we want the answer to be and what the truth is, is one and the same," Norman said firmly. "Enough of this. If you guys don't want to look into it, I'll do it myself. One way or another, the truth about Bigfoot will come out—and I'm going to be the one to show the world that he's real."

# CHAPTER SIX

Tulia gave Emmerson her number when she parted ways with the group outside the diner. She wasn't really sure what to do next. Thea had invited her to come along with them, but she still wasn't comfortable with the idea of sneaking back to the scene of the attack. She didn't want to leave yet, since the investigation was ongoing, but she had somewhat lost her taste for hiking, even if she went to a different forest. She didn't believe in Bigfoot, of course, but what she believed in and what she worried about when she was alone in a dark forest wasn't always the same thing.

Finally, she decided to stick with her original plan. She would head out toward the coast, spend some time at the Tillamook Creamery and then go to the beach. She'd go get her RV first; she wanted the freedom to camp somewhere near the coast if she didn't feel like returning tonight.

Satisfied with her plans, she returned to her RV, turned on her GPS, and headed out with Cicero happily watching the landscape go by outside the window. With an hour drive ahead of her, she turned on her music and did her best to relax. Oregon really was one of the most beautiful states she'd seen so far, but she thought that about almost every new state she visited. Once she got through the Willamette Valley and the state forest, the landscape flattened out a bit. It was mostly farm country, and she spotted a lot of cows.

When she arrived at the Tillamook Creamery, it was busy enough that she had to park in the lot across the street. Leaving some soft music on for Cicero, she crossed the road and joined the line waiting to get into the creamery. She opted for a self-tour, and on her way out, bought a big block of cheese. She'd had Tillamook cheese before, of course, but there was something neat about buying it right from the source.

It felt nice to do something that was just … fun. Touristy and fun. No thinking about murders, and while she enjoyed hiking, it was nice not to have to slog through mud, branches, and the various other unpleasant aspects of being outside. *I should do this more often,* she thought as she went back to the RV. *I've been living the RV life for a while. Maybe I should stay in hotels more, and experience some of the big cities out here.*

Her plans for the day were already settled, though. The coast wasn't far away, so once she was back at her RV, she typed a quick search into her phone and found the closest beach, which was at Cape Meares. The road took her in a long loop through a natural coastal area like nothing she had ever seen before, even having grown up going to the Great Lakes.

As soon as she rounded the next curve, she could see the ocean, and the sight took her breath away. With her windows down to let the smell of the ocean in, she drove slowly down a residential road, looking at all the houses, some of which were quaint and some of which were modern, but all of which had an amazing view of the beach and the ocean. She wondered what it would be like to live so close to the ocean, to be able to look out her door every day and see the view. Would she ever get bored of it?

Finally, she reached a sandy parking lot, with a path that led down a short hill through tall seagrass to the beach.

She parked and then grabbed Cicero's harness out

of the center console and took him out of his cage to put it on him.

"Ready to see the ocean, buddy?" she asked.

Stepping out of the RV, with Cicero on her hand, she took a deep breath. The ocean breeze tugged at her hair. She carefully made her way down the sandy path to the beach proper, to where the white-capped waves were lapping at the shore. The sound of the surf was a steady roar, and in the distance, a spire of rock was rearing its head from the water. To her left, a distance down the beach, she saw a rocky cliff with pine trees clinging to the top. Cicero gave the seabirds that were wheeling around in the air above them a distrustful glance, then spread his wings, seeming to enjoy the wind coming off the sea.

"This is amazing," she breathed, walking along the beach. As she got closer to the water, she noticed strange, gelatinous circles on the sand, and after a moment of confusion, realized they were jellyfish. A black bird of some sort was walking along the beach not far from her, one that she'd never seen before. What was it? Maybe some sort of cormorant?

She turned to look back at the houses that were lining the beach and felt a surge of longing. She wanted to live somewhere like this. Maybe she would get tired of it eventually, but she couldn't imagine it happening any time soon.

She walked on the beach for over an hour, taking off her shoes and going close enough to the water that the chilly waves could lap at her feet. Finally, on her way back to the RV with her sandals looped through her pinky finger and Cicero on her shoulder, she gave a satisfied sigh. This was the perfect vacation day. She should make a point of doing touristy things more often. They were touristy for a reason—because they were fun.

The wind and the roar of the surf was loud enough that she almost didn't realize that the faint jingling sound she was hearing was coming from her phone, which was shoved into her back pocket. Finally realizing that the noise was coming from her, she took the phone out and saw her mother's name on the caller ID. It was the middle of a weekday, which meant her parents would usually be at work, so she was slightly concerned as she answered it, turning the volume up and pressing the phone to her ear.

"Mom? Is everything all right?"

"I'm fine, sweetie," her mother said. "What's that noise?"

"I'm at the ocean."

"Oh, how nice. Please send me some pictures?"

"I will," Tulia promised. She walked over to large piece of driftwood—a log, really—and sat down on it, trying to focus on the call. "What's going on?"

"A man just came by my office," her mom said. "He said he was looking for you."

Tulia's stomach swooped. "Did he say who he was?"

"He said he was a private investigator. He didn't tell us much more than that, but I wasn't sure what to do. I told him I wasn't sure where you were right now, but I don't think he believed me. He finally left when my boss came out and threatened to call the police."

"Luis has been hiring private investigators trying to find me," Tulia said. Most of the happy, contented feeling from earlier was gone. "I'm sorry, Mom. I didn't think they'd start bothering you."

"Don't worry about me," her mother said. "It's you I'm worried about. Are you okay? What's going to happen if they find you?"

"I don't know, but probably nothing good." She sighed, then quickly added, "I don't think I'm in danger or anything, but Luis is kicking up a stink about that lottery money. He seems to think he deserves some."

"Still? I'm sorry, sweetie. If your dad or I can help, let us know."

"I will," Tulia said. "Thanks for telling me. I love you. I'm gonna get going now, but I'll send you pictures of the ocean once I get back to the RV."

She ended the call and shoved the phone back into her pocket angrily. She stomped through the sand, climbing the short hill to the parking area. *Luis.* Why couldn't he just leave her alone? She didn't know what he was planning—as far as she was aware, he had no legal claim to any of her money, but he must have something up his sleeve.

Climbing into the RV, she took Cicero's harness off and put him back in his cage, then gave him part of a banana so he could snack while she thought about what to do next. After opening the windows so the fresh sea air could come in through the screens, she flopped down on her couch and took her phone out, staring at it. She was tempted to call Luis and tell him to leave her alone, but she hadn't spoken with him often since they broke up and had no real desire to start now. Instead, she found another name on her contact list and hit the call button. A man answered after a few rings.

"Hey, Samuel," she said. "Do you have time to talk?"

"Sure," he said. "Hold on a second."

She heard a sound, like a car door closing, then he said, "How are you doing? Where are you at now?"

"I'm on the Oregon coast, not far from the Tillamook Creamery."

"Oh, really?" he asked. "I'm not far from you, then."

"Where are you?" she asked. She knew Samuel had been planning on taking a road trip himself as a way to recover after being kidnapped and nearly killed by a serial killer. He was a private investigator, and one of the better ones, but had managed to land himself in a heap of trouble during his last job.

"I'm in Portland," he said. "I've got some cousins in the city who I never see, since I'm usually on the other side of the country from them, so I figured since I was only a couple states away and wasn't planning on going home yet, I might as well come out and visit. Would you like to meet up?"

She wasn't an expert on Oregon's geography, but she thought Portland was about an hour to an hour and a half away. She'd been camping about twenty minutes away from the city, so she had an idea of where it was. "How about dinner?" she asked, thinking she could return to her old campsite and have some time to get ready before going out. "I'd love to see you. There's something I need to ask your advice on, anyway."

"Great. I'll get some restaurant recommendations from my cousin. I'll see you soon."

She ended the call with a smile on her face. She had been intending on asking Samuel for advice about how to deal with the private investigator who was trying to find her, but seeing him would be even better.

## CHAPTER SEVEN

She returned to her old RV site and hooked everything back up, then pulled the blinds shut and turned on the lights inside before digging through all the clothes she had brought. It wasn't a date, and she knew that, but she wanted to look nice. She was looking forward to an excuse to feel pretty again.

Finally, she settled on a dark blue sundress that had small white dots on it. It wasn't her normal style, but she had bought it earlier that year and hadn't had a chance to wear it yet. When she tried it on, it still fit her perfectly.

She showered and dried her hair, then did her hair up in a loose braid. It was getting long; she'd have to find a hair salon soon. She kept her makeup simple and subtle—she wasn't going clubbing, she was going to a restaurant with a guy who was sort of, maybe a friend, and nothing more. After putting on a pair of flats that complemented her dress, she looked at herself in the mirror. She looked … nice. Surprisingly nice. She was more tanned now than she had been when she left for her trip, and even though she hadn't exactly been eating healthy all the time, she had been exercising a lot more, and it showed at the backs of her arms and in her calves. Even the way she held herself was different. She looked more confident, even just looking at herself in the mirror.

"All right," she said to herself. "Time to go. Cicero, I'm going to go out for dinner—definitely not on a date—so you stay here, all right, honey?" She turned to her bird, who looked content to sleep. It was evening, and he'd had a busy day.

Before she left, she put the shade up in the windshield to prevent people from looking in. When she turned off the lights, the inside was dimly lit by the evening light coming in through the shades, making it look cozy. It was the perfect place for a nap. She felt bad leaving Cicero alone, but at least she knew he would sleep the whole time.

She was just double-checking that she had everything she wanted in her purse when someone knocked on the RV's door.

She jumped, not expecting anyone, then got up to answer it, assuming it was someone from a neighboring RV spot who needed help with something. She was not expecting to open the door and see Norman standing there.

"What are you doing here?" she asked, the words coming out more unfriendly than she had intended. She looked around for the others, but it was just him. "And how did you find me?"

"I heard Emmerson tell you about this place," he said, pulling back a little and looking somewhat hurt by her greeting. "Emmerson refused to give me your number—he said he didn't want me to pester you—but I need to ask you something."

"Right," she said, trying to run her fingers through her hair before she remembered it was in a braid. "Well, come on in."

She stepped back, and he came into the RV. She gestured at the couch. "Go ahead and take a seat if you want."

"This won't take long," he said. "I just want to know if you would be willing to do a post on your blog about what happened in the woods."

She blinked. "My blog?"

"I know you have quite a few followers," he said. "If you can get the word out—"

"No, wait, how do you know about my blog?" she asked. "I know I didn't tell you about it." She never told anyone about the blog until she trusted them, since she had mentioned her lottery winnings in it.

Norman looked to the side, wincing. "Look, it was Thea's idea. Emmerson backed her up. It wasn't my idea. They both wanted to do a more thorough investigation, to make sure there was no way what happened to Mason could have been murder. And since you're the one who found the crime scene, well…"

"You did some digging into me to see if there was any reason I might have killed Mason?" she asked with a sigh. "I guess I can't blame you for that."

"Look, I know you are a skeptic, but I really think we have something here. If you do a blog post, you might get more people to come out with stories about their experiences with Bigfoot. It could really help us out, especially if we get locals to come forward. We're trying to do something here that could change everything we know about the world."

"I'm not comfortable talking about an active investigation on my blog," she said. "It's a personal policy. I don't like the thought that the killer might stumble upon it and use the information I provide to dodge the law."

"Somehow, I don't think Bigfoot has access to WiFi, so you wouldn't have to worry about that."

She glared at him until he laughed, raising his hands. "Kidding, kidding. Look, you don't even need to talk about the murder—maybe just talk about what you saw out there? The smell, the hair, the prints… With your reach, we might actually be able to get solid evidence."

"I'll think about it," she promised. "Look, I've got to go. I'm meeting someone for dinner."

"Okay, I'll get out of your hair. Think about it, though, all right?"

They left the RV together. She expected him to get back into his car and go, but first he said, "Here, I'll give you my number."

She accepted it, though she was pretty certain she had already made up her mind not to post anything about Bigfoot on her blog. "Are you guys still planning on going to Mason and Melody's campsite?"

He hesitated. "I'd rather not say. I know you're against it."

"I understand. Just … be careful. Someone … or something," she admitted reluctantly, "killed Mason. I don't know what or who it was, but if it's still out there, I don't want you guys to get hurt."

"We will be," he promised. "I hope you have a

good time on your date." He raised one hand in farewell and began to walk away.

"It's not a date," she called after him, then sighed, turning her attention back to her sedan. Date or not, if she didn't hurry up, she was going to be late.

# CHAPTER EIGHT

The restaurant Samuel had chosen for dinner was in downtown Portland. Tulia took in the city as she drove, admiring the amount of greenery she saw. Once she arrived, she parked in a lot behind the building, then walked around to the front, letting herself into the restaurant.

“I’m meeting someone,” she told the hostess, spotting Samuel and gesturing toward where he was seated at a table for two against the back wall.

“Go on back,” the hostess said with a smile. “I’ll let your server know you’re here.”

She felt her heart rate increase a bit as she walked through the restaurant toward Samuel. It was a nice place, with dim lighting and food that looked delicious, judging by what she saw on other people's plates as she passed by. This wasn't a date … was it?

"Hey," she said with a smile once she reached his table. He looked a lot more laid-back than usual, though she supposed that made sense, since he was on vacation now. He was wearing light blue jeans and a green polo shirt, with his hair slicked back in his usual style. He rose and almost gave her a hug but then stopped himself and shook hands with her.

"I hope this place is all right," he said. "It had good reviews online, and my cousin said he and his wife liked it when they came here last year."

She laughed, taking her seat across from him as he sat back down. "Everything looks great. I'm hungry." She hadn't eaten since brunch, and that had been a while ago.

"How long have you been in the state?"

"A few days," she said, sipping the glass of water that was already waiting for her. "I wasn't planning on being around much longer, but I got held up. I'll tell you about it after we've had a chance to look over the menu."

When the waitress came, she ordered a drink, and she and Samuel kept their chat light as they both perused the dinner menu. She was hungry, and finally settled on getting a surf and turf dish with lobster tail, steak, garlic mashed potatoes, and asparagus. It was expensive, but she didn't have to worry about the price anymore. It still felt strange to order it, since she never would have before. Would she ever get used to her new life? In a way, she hoped she didn't. She liked feeling a thrill whenever she remembered just how much she had won with that lucky lottery ticket.

Once their order was in, Samuel leaned forward a bit. "So, what's going on? You must've called me for a reason, and you sounded upset when you first answered."

She took a deep breath. "I'm having problems with another private investigative agency, one my ex hired…" she began.

She told him the whole story. She had already mentioned some of the issues she'd been having with Luis, but she was more thorough this time, telling him about all of the calls she had been getting, and the harassing comments on her blog. The last straw was the private investigator visiting her mother at work. "It's getting to the point where I'm really just not all right with it. Is there something I can do to stop this? Even if Luis does find me, it's not like I'm going to just give up and give him the money, so I don't know why he's trying so hard to find me. We weren't married or anything. He doesn't have any claim to it. I don't know what his plan is, but going after my parents is too far."

"You could try calling the agency and explaining the situation to them, if you can figure out who he hired," Samuel mused. "But the only surefire way would be to take it to court and get a court order to stop the harassment. You might have to return to Michigan to do that, though; I'm not sure."

She sighed. "Great. Do you think it would be best if I just called him and tried to figure it out between the two of us?"

"Is he the sort of guy who would be reasonable about something like this?"

"I doubt it."

"Hmm. Is he well off, this Luis?"

"No, not really," she said. "He makes a decent hourly wage but is pretty bad at managing his money."

"Your best bet is probably just waiting until he runs out of funds, then." Samuel grinned at her. "We don't come cheap. Some agencies will give discounts for the sort of thing Marc and I were hired to do—tracking down a killer and helping bereaved family members. We're not all cold and heartless. But something like this, yeah, I can tell you that agency is probably charging him as much as they can."

"So, I've just got to wait," she said with a sigh. "Thanks, I guess it's better to know my options even if none of them are good."

"I can look into it for you if you want," he said. "Not to brag, but I am kind of good at digging into things. I could probably at least figure out what agency he's working with, then you could try talking to them."

She laughed. "No, don't worry about it. You're on vacation."

"I don't mind," he said. "I feel like I owe you for how much Marc and I freaked you out back when we were following you through Michigan and Wisconsin. I'll do some digging. I'll let you know when I turn something up."

"Thank you," she said. "I'll owe you one. Let me get dinner."

"No, it's my treat," he said with a wave of his hand. "I'm the one who invited you out here."

"I can't let you pay—"

She broke off as her phone started ringing in her purse. Wincing, she took it out and hit the volume button to silence the call. "Sorry about that. I've gotten out of the habit of keeping it on vibrate."

"I don't mind," he said. "You can go ahead and answer it."

"I've honestly got no idea who it is," she said, staring at the number on the screen. "The number looks kind of familiar. My phone says it's from Oregon." She frowned. "Hold on, it might be the hospital calling." She had given Melody her number, and it was possible that the woman might need something.

"The hospital?" Samuel asked, concerned, but she was already pressing the button to answer.

"Hello?"

"Hi, Tulia?" The voice was female and sounded frightened.

"Melody?"

"No, it's Thea. Something happened. Emmerson's missing, and Norman is about to take off into the woods. I don't know what to do."

"Slow down. What's going on?"

"Something attacked our camp," Thea said. "Everything is a mess. And … there's prints, Tulia, footprints and clumps of fur everywhere. I don't know if it's the same thing you saw or not, but I'm really freaked out. I don't know what to do."

"Are you saying Bigfoot attacked your camp?"

Tulia asked, frowning. Across the table, Samuel gave her an odd look.

"I know you won't believe me, but I don't know who else to call. Norman will be mad if I call the police, but I don't know what else to do. Someone needs to come talk some sense into him. He's about to go into the woods after it, and I'm afraid he's going to get hurt."

"I'm in the middle of a da—dinner right now," Tulia said, wincing as the word 'date' almost left her lips. "I can't come out—"

Samuel reached over and touched her wrist. Frowning, she asked Thea to hold on for a second and muted the call. "What?"

"I know I'm missing a lot of context here, but if there's been a Bigfoot sighting nearby, I wouldn't mind looking into it."

She stared at him. "Are you telling me you believe in Bigfoot too?"

"No," he said. "But I've always found the whole phenomenon fascinating. I'd love to actually see the scene of a supposed sighting firsthand and take a look at the evidence people find so convincing."

She sighed and unmuted the call.

"All right," she said to Thea. "We can be out there in

about half an hour, maybe forty-five minutes at most. We just have to wait for our food so we can take it to go."

She was not missing out on her lobster and steak for this. "Tell Norman to wait. If he wants to go chasing after Bigfoot, well, I've got someone who's willing to help."

# CHAPTER NINE

Thea and her group were still camping in the same state forest where Melody and Mason had been attacked, though they were a few miles farther down the road at a primitive campground. Tulia hadn't planned on coming back to this area anytime soon, and felt a sour feeling in her stomach as soon as she pulled in. She wished she'd told the other woman she was unavailable, and that her group would have to figure things out for themselves.

Shooting a quick glance at the text Thea had sent her, she followed the directions and took the bumpy dirt trail down toward the very last campsite. There were only a few other campers at the campground, and none seemed to have ventured so far back on the increasingly bad path.

Finally, she found the last campsite, which was undoubtably the one the cryptid hunters were staying at. There were three tents in the small clearing, along with an old, beat-up truck. Two of the three tents had collapsed, and there was garbage spread out across the clearing.

Tulia pulled to a stop next to the truck, and Samuel parked next to her in his rental car. Through the window, he met her eyes and raised an eyebrow. She hadn't had much time to catch him up on things; right now, all he knew was that she had somehow fallen in with a group of people who thought Bigfoot was real and were out to prove it.

She'd have to explain the whole story to him eventually, but now wasn't the time. Thea was already approaching her car, her hair a frazzled mess.

Tulia stepped out of the vehicle, hearing Samuel do the same behind her. Thea was wringing her hands as she drew closer.

"Thank goodness you came. I really don't know what to do."

"Tell me what happened," Tulia said. "I'm not sure how I'll be able to help."

"Well, I was in my—" She broke off, glancing at Samuel as he came to stand next to Tulia. "I'm sorry, who are you?"

"I told you I was bringing someone." She gestured at him. "Thea, this is Samuel, a … well, a friend of mine. He's also a private investigator. I'm not really sure what's going on, but he'll probably be more help than I am."

"A private investigator, really?" Thea bit her lip. "Look, Tulia, you know what we do. People like him don't take us seriously."

"I'll keep any doubts I have private," Samuel promised. He reached out to shake her hand. "I'm just here to keep Tulia company. I won't judge. Heck, I used to be a big fan of the Sasquatch when I was younger."

Thea shook his hand, then took a deep breath. "Right. Well, I was in my tent, just relaxing. It's been a long couple of days—a lot of hiking around, you know?—and I was hoping to get a nap in before we headed back out into the woods tonight."

"You guys go into the woods at night?" Tulia asked. It didn't sound appealing to her.

"We've got some night vision equipment, and Norman thought we might have a better chance of catching something at night. Anyway, I was resting when I heard something. It was a roar, that's the only way I can describe it. It was like nothing I've ever heard before. And then … it attacked."

"Did you see it?" Tulia asked, drawn in despite herself. She realized the same heavy animal stench she'd smelled at Melody and Mason's campsite hung in the air.

Thea nodded, her eyes wide. "I know you're not going to believe me, but it was him. It was Bigfoot. I swear. As soon as I heard it start wrecking our camp, I came out of my tent, and I saw this huge furry thing tearing through the tents and throwing everything around. I freaked out and hid in the truck until I couldn't hear anything anymore."

"On the phone you said Emmerson is missing. Do you think that … whatever did this to your camp hurt him?" Tulia looked around. She was unwilling to entertain the idea of Bigfoot going on a killing spree, but something about the animal smell that clung to everything raised the hair on the back of her neck. It was hard *not* to believe when some primitive part of her was screaming at her that there was a big, dangerous creature nearby.

"I don't think so. He and Norman weren't in camp; they were off in the woods setting up trail cams. Norman came rushing back when I started yelling for them, but we couldn't find Emmerson. Norman is convinced that Bigfoot hurt him."

Samuel left his place at her side and started carefully picking his way through camp. Tulia watched him as she spoke to Thea.

"Where's Norman now?"

"He left!" Thea's voice cracked, and she sniffed. "I begged him to wait, but he said he was going with or without me. He left me alone here."

"He went to look for the missing man?" Samuel asked. He was crouching down a few feet away from them, taking a picture of something on the ground with his phone.

"Yes," Thea said. "He loaded up all his gear and told me he wasn't coming back until he found Emmerson or Bigfoot—or both."

Tulia blew out a long breath. She felt … overwhelmed. "You really should have called the police, not me. I don't know what you want me to do." She didn't mention that Thea had interrupted her dinner with Samuel; there was no point in making the other woman feel bad when she was already so obviously upset.

"I thought he'd wait, that you'd be able to talk some sense into him." Thea kicked at a loose stick. "Now he and Emmerson are both gone, who knows where in this huge forest. Shoot, maybe we *should* call the police. Norman's going to be mad, but I don't think I'm overreacting at this point."

"Tulia, come over here and take a look at this," Samuel called out.

Glad for the distraction, since she wasn't sure how to respond to Thea in a way that wouldn't just make the situation worse, Tulia walked over to him and crouched down to look at the thing he was pointing at. It was a huge footprint, just like the one she had seen at Melody and Mason's camp. There was a tuft of brown hair sticking out of the mud inside it, like it had been stepped on.

"I saw those at the other campsite too," she said. "I don't know what to think at this point."

Both his eyebrows rose. "You'll have to give me the full story soon. There's definitely something going on, and I'd be lying if I said I wasn't intrigued. I want to look into this, but our first priority should be to find the missing man. Or men."

"Right. I'll talk to Thea about calling the police or maybe the park serv—" She broke off when she heard the sound of snapping sticks. She and Samuel rose to their feet together, and when she looked in the direction of the sound, she spotted movement within the shadows of the trees across the clearing from where they were standing.

"It's coming back!" Thea screamed. "It's going to kill us! Oh my—Norman?"

Tulia realized she was clinging to Samuel's arm and let go, staring at the man who stumbled out of the trees. This wasn't the Norman she'd seen before. This man looked terrified. He had a smear of blood on his forearm and more on his hands, and his jeans were ripped. He stumbled out of the forest toward them, his eyes glued to Thea.

"We need to call an ambulance," he gasped. "I found Emmerson. He's hurt. He won't wake up."

# CHAPTER TEN

Two hours later, Tulia found herself back at the same hospital where she had visited Melody just hours ago. This time, the cryptid hunting team—or what remained of them—was much more shaken. Norman was sitting hunched over in a chair in the hospital waiting room, staring at his hands as if he could still see the blood on them. Thea was next to him, wrapped in a blanket one of the hospital staff had found for her. She was staring blankly off into the distance.

Tulia and Samuel were a few chairs away from them, and while they were a bit less shaken simply because they hadn't known Emmerson as well, the mood was somber.

"I wish we knew if he would be all right," Tulia murmured, not for the first time.

She'd watched the rescue team carry Emmerson out of the woods on a stretcher. He'd still been bleeding from his head wound, and had been frighteningly limp. He was alive, though, and she told herself they had to cling to that. At least he had a chance, unlike Mason.

"We're not going to learn anything by sitting here," Samuel told her gently. "We're not relatives. I doubt they'll even give any information out to his friends. I'm sorry, I know it's hard to not know, but we'll just have to wait for them to call you as soon as someone tells them how he's doing."

"I know." She took a deep breath, trying to calm herself down. "I'm sorry. I didn't mean to drag you into something like this."

"I'd still like to hear the full story, but I'm not upset. If you're going to be in danger, I'd rather be around to help you out of it." He looked slightly embarrassed and quickly added, "I'd want to help anyone, of course. It's the right thing to do."

She gave him a weak smile, but her heart wasn't in it. She knew he was right; sitting around in the waiting room wasn't going to achieve anything. She and Samuel wouldn't get answers out of the doctors and nurses who had to keep their patients' confidentiality. But there was one other person who might be able to give them more information.

"I'll say goodbye to Norman and Thea, then do you want to go with me to visit someone else in the hospital?" she asked him quietly.

He raised an eyebrow. "Just how many people do you know in this place?"

"Just the two," she promised him, almost smiling at the absurdity of it. "I'll be right back. I'll start explaining while we're in the elevator."

She rose to walk over to Thea and Norman. Thea's eyes moved over to her, but she didn't say anything. Norman didn't even seem to notice her.

"I'm going to head out," she said softly, directing her words to both of them. "I know you're dealing with a lot, but if you can, I'd be grateful if you'd let me know when you hear something."

"We will," Thea whispered. "Thanks for trying to help."

"Anytime," Tulia said. She felt bad for her earlier resentment. Right now, she just wanted everyone to be okay.

As if reading her mind, Norman looked up at her suddenly. "He'll be okay. He'll wake up."

"I hope so."

"He has to," Norman said. "That's all there is to it."

She hoped it would be that simple. Leaving them to continue to wait for their friend, she gestured Samuel over to the elevator, where she hit the button for the third floor. It was late; visiting hours were almost over, but she thought they'd have just enough time to drop in on Melody.

"So, how, exactly, did you get involved in all of this?" Samuel asked as the doors slid shut in front of them.

"Cicero and I were hiking when I heard a scream…" she began.

She got to finding Melody after seeing the camp and Mason's body by the time the elevator dinged and the door opened onto the third floor, and quickly told him about stumbling across the cryptid group on the trail after realizing just how lost she was.

"You know there isn't actually a Sasquatch out there attacking people, right?" he asked when she was done.

"Of course." She wrinkled her nose. "I mean, I can see how a superstitious person might … but there's got to be something else going on. Maybe a rogue bear."

"Those weren't bear prints we saw at their campsite," Samuel said. "It was too humanoid. It looked like a great ape print."

"But if it's not Bigfoot—"

"Oh, it's a Sasquatch print," Samuel said. "It's just as real as all of the other ones people have found over the years. Just like the rest of them, this one was left by a person, not a big hairy ape. This is a very, very dedicated attempt at a false Sasquatch sighting, and whoever is behind it is a murderer."

His statement left an uncomfortable silence behind. Tulia knew he was right—she'd been clinging desperately to the hope it was a bear gone wrong—but the thought of a person dressed up in a Bigfoot costume and running around in the huge state forest attacking people was disturbing.

Clearing her throat, she nodded at Melody's door as they approached it. "Well, this is where she is. The last time I spoke with her, she thought her boyfriend, Mason, was killed in a Bigfoot attack. She's still got to be in shock from what happened; I don't think it would be right to argue the point with her."

"Of course," Samuel said. "I can't imagine what she's going through. I won't say anything about the attack, period."

Tulia nodded, then raised her hand to knock on

the door, which was shut. She waited a moment, then, when there was no response, she knocked again.

"That's weird. I wonder if she's asleep."

"They must have moved her to somewhere else," Samuel said. "Look, there's a sign."

In a wall mount next to the door was a plastic card that read *Vacant: Dirty*. Tulia stared at it for a second, then pushed down the handle, opening the door slowly.

The bed inside the room was empty, and all of Melody's things were gone.

# CHAPTER ELEVEN

They still had their food from the restaurant in their cars, and since Samuel was staying with his cousin, Tulia invited him back to her RV so they could reheat their food and eat it while they talked.

With Cicero watching from his perch and one of the window shades pulled up just enough so she could crack the window for some fresh air, she launched back into the story of the Bigfoot attack and everything that had happened since. It was satisfying to be able to share the story with someone. Especially since, while Samuel was interested, he didn't try to convince her that Bigfoot was real—or even believe it was a possibility.

"I don't know how you find yourself in these sorts of situations," he said, shaking his head. "You shouldn't have gone toward a scream when you were out alone in the woods. You could have gotten hurt."

"You know I'm not the sort of person who can let someone else be hurt or killed just because I was too afraid to act," she said. "And you're not really in a position to say anything about it, either."

"I know," he said, sighing. "I owe you. That's another reason you should let me look into the issue you're having with the private investigator your ex hired."

She shook her head. "I didn't mean it like that. You don't owe me anything. I'm just saying… I've helped people in the past. I know what I can do. How could I ever walk away if I know I could have done something to help someone?"

"Well, next time that happens, just be aware that you might stumble headfirst into the Loch Ness monster. Oh, you're from Michigan—maybe you'll come across the Dogman."

She rolled her eyes. "Okay, I'm not going to deny that there might have been a few minutes when I first came across the campsite that I wondered… But you and I both know there's no such thing as Bigfoot. And you said the tracks weren't from a bear."

He nodded, more serious now. "Someone's behind this. A human. And they've already killed one person.

I don't see how this could possibly end without someone else getting hurt. Look what happened to Emmerson."

She nodded, biting her lip. Emmerson had been her favorite out of the cryptid hunting team—mostly because he shared her skepticism—and she was horrified that he'd been injured so badly. She hated that there was nothing she could do to help him. All she could do was hope that he would wake up, and that he would be okay.

"Well, the police are already investigating the murder," she said. "And I'm sure someone is looking into what happened to Emmerson too. What should *we* do?"

He sighed. "You're not going to like it, but I don't think we should do anything. This isn't our job, Tulia. Even as a private investigator, getting involved in murder investigations is messy. I've seen a lot of bad detectives completely derail cases. Even the good ones all too often end up destroying evidence or getting hurt themselves. Sometimes it's best just to step back and let the people with the correct resources to do this properly get their work done."

She hesitated. She knew he had a point. She, especially, would just get in the way. But… "What if I hired you?" she suggested. "Then it *would* be your job to figure out what happened."

He raised an eyebrow. "I'm afraid it's a job I wouldn't be able to take. First of all, you have to go through the agency I work for. Second of all, I'm on vacation. I was just almost killed in the course of investigating another murder. I'm all for helping catch the bad guy, but I only do it on the clock. And I've got a lot of vacation days saved up."

"Sorry. I shouldn't have asked. I know you earned your vacation. It's just frustrating. Am I supposed to just … walk away from all this?"

"Sometimes you have to," he said. "My advice would be to try to contact your friend tomorrow, the one who left before we could visit her, and make sure she's okay, and maybe check in with Emmerson's team to see how he's doing. Then, climb into the driver's seat and head off to your next destination. Taking a road trip around the country by yourself, especially as a woman, is dangerous enough. There is no reason to go looking for ways to make it even more dangerous."

Morosely, she poked at her surf and turf meal. It was good, but it would've been even better if she hadn't had to microwave it to reheat it. Even though she was hungry, she was beginning to feel too depressed to have much of an appetite.

"I guess you're right," she said at last. "I need to learn to let things go."

"You're one of the luckiest people I know," Samuel said. "But luck doesn't last forever, and you've already used up a heck of a lot of yours. You're supposed to be enjoying yourself. Why don't you tell me what else you've gotten up to since we parted ways in Montana? What have you been doing? Where are you going next?"

She was glad for the opportunity to change the topic, and gave him a short rundown of her adventures up until this point. She was telling him about her decision to spend some time exploring city life, since she'd had more than her fill of nature recently, when her phone began to ring again.

Groaning, she got up to take it out of her purse where she had left it on the counter. "I'm pretty sure the surf and turf meal is cursed. That's two times now I've been interrupted—" She broke off as she stared at the number on the screen. She hadn't saved Thea's number the last time she called, but she recognized it. "It's Thea," she said. "It might be about Emmerson."

"Go ahead. I'm not about to get in the way of an important call."

Feeling nervous, she hit the button to answer the call and pressed the phone to her ear. "Hello?"

"Tulia, thank goodness," Thea said. "Are you okay?"

"Yeah, I'm fine. What's going on? How's Emmerson?"

"He still hasn't woken up, but that's not what I'm calling about," the other woman said. "It's Melody. She left the hospital."

"Oh, I already know that," Tulia said, sitting back down across from Samuel. "We went to see her before we left, but all her things were already gone."

"We talked to the nurse on her level, and she said the police had been questioning Melody just a few minutes before she left. Melody didn't sign out or see the doctor first. She just walked herself out. Norman managed to get the nurse to tell us what she overheard. The officer told Melody they were treating Mason's death as a homicide, and she left *right after.* Tulia, I'm worried she might have killed him. I wanted to let you know in case she tries to contact you. If she asks you for help, think twice. She could be dangerous. Norman is out looking for her now. Be careful."

"I will," Tulia said, her brow furrowing. "Thanks for calling, Thea. Take care."

She ended the call and looked back up at Samuel. She told him what Thea had told her, then said, "It doesn't feel right, though. Melody, the murderer? It can't be her. She was still in the hospital when someone attacked Emmerson."

"Maybe she's working with—" Samuel broke off as something struck the RV hard enough to make it rock. Cicero squawked and fluttered off his perch in shock. Crouching down to pick him up, Tulia ran a soothing hand down his feathers, then turned to Samuel, her eyes wide.

"What on earth was that?" Before he could respond, something roared just outside the window loudly enough to make both of them wince and Cicero to whistle in alarm. The roar was followed by another thud, and the heavy, musky scent of animal wafted in through the window.

All of a sudden, Tulia thought she might believe in Bigfoot after all.

# CHAPTER TWELVE

Tulia hurried to put Cicero in his cage, hoping the bars would keep him safe from whatever was attacking the RV. Then, she dug through her purse until she found her pepper spray. Holding it up, she turned to Samuel. He'd picked up the knife she'd used to cut the banana for Cicero earlier.

"Does this thing have any cameras on the outside?" he shouted over the sound of the thudding, which had become constant.

"It does!"

She wouldn't have thought of it herself. She hurried to the front of the RV, where the sunshade was still up, and started the electronics without turning the entire engine on. It took her a few tries to find the exterior cameras—she hadn't really used them except for parking—but finally, she pulled up the cameras on the console screen. The RV had 360° cameras all around it, which were very helpful when she was trying to park in a narrow space, but were even more helpful right now, when they were trying to figure out what manner of monster was trying to kill them.

The camera showed movement on only one side of the RV; the side with the window that was cracked open, near the kitchen table. She clicked on that image to enlarge it, and she and Samuel both stared at the image of a large, hairy beast ramming its shoulder against the RV again and again. Suddenly, the monster paused, and another earsplitting roar threatened to make her ears bleed.

"I'm seeing things. Please tell me I'm seeing things, Samuel."

"It's a costume," he said, straightening up. "There's no way that's real."

She stared. It was a very convincing costume. Granted, the cameras weren't at the best angle and weren't the highest definition, but still, it was hard to see what that hunched, hairy form had in common with a human.

Samuel pulled out his phone and started punching something into it, but Tulia grabbed his wrist, bringing his attention back to the cameras. She hit the back button to go to the surround view again, because the monster had disappeared off the camera she had been looking at.

"It's going around to the other side!"

"It is the door—" Samuel broke off as the RV's door was yanked open.

Tulia screamed, and Samuel braced himself in front of her, holding the knife up even though it seemed like a pitiful defense against the creature that was looking up at them. It smelled rancid this close, and seemed to fill the entire entrance to the RV. It roared again, and the sound was deafening.

Tulia raised her pepper spray, but didn't want to spray it here. First of all, she and Samuel were likely to get caught in the mist as well in such a small area, and secondly—and most importantly—she had no idea what the spray would do to Cicero.

It was the moment of hesitation that gave her the time to realize something was wrong. The monster had roared, but its mouth hadn't moved. And now that she was looking at it closely, the eyes were blank and hollow, as if they were part of a mask.

Come to think of it, the monster looked weirdly familiar…

"That's not even a Bigfoot costume," she

managed to get out. "It's a Wookiee costume!"

Just like that, the spell was broken. Tulia could pick out all the other hints that it was a costume. The roar they'd been hearing must have been a recording. Whatever that animal smell was, it must have been purchased from a hunting store.

"Who are you?" Samuel demanded. "Take off the mask."

She was certain that wasn't going to work; whoever this was seemed dedicated to their role as a Sasquatch. She remembered Thea's warning, but … it couldn't be Melody, could it? She bit her lip. She didn't want to believe that the woman she'd helped save was a killer, but even she could admit that it almost made sense.

Until she realized that the person in the costume was standing up straight, and had moved with no limp. It couldn't be Melody. She wouldn't have been able to fool the doctors at the hospital into believing she had a broken ankle if she didn't, and there was no way she could be moving around so easily with that sort of injury.

Then who… She inhaled sharply. Of course. It all made sense. *He'd* gone into the woods after Emmerson, only for the other man to come out barely alive. *He* was obsessed with the Bigfoot legend. He was the only one she could imagine being this dedicated to the whole charade.

"Norman," she said, taking a step forward and pushing past Samuel. "I know that's you. You can end the charade now. Neither of us are fooled."

Reaching up, the monster pulled at its face, taking off its mask. Even though she'd already known, she still gasped again when she saw Norman's face. His eyes were wide and wild.

"I suppose the costume works better when you're alone and afraid in the woods," Norman said after staring at her for a second. "I wonder if anyone would believe me if I said I saw a Sasquatch shoot two people with a gun." He reached into his suit with one oversized fur glove and withdrew a handgun, which he held awkwardly in the costume's gloved hand. "It doesn't matter. If I spin the story right, the details will get lost. Three Bigfoot attacks in the same stretch of forest in less than three days' time. This is going to make worldwide news."

"I don't understand," Tulia said, keeping the pepper spray in front of her. Her eyes flicked from the gun back up to his face, but she held her stance. "I thought you were looking for evidence Bigfoot was real. How does faking these attacks help?"

"I want people to believe me," he said. "If people start believing in Bigfoot, though, more people will start looking for him, and eventually, someone will find him."

"You're really willing to kill people over this?" she asked, aghast.

To her surprise, he hesitated. "I didn't mean to kill the first guy. I didn't think I'd even hit him; I just wanted to scare him when I threw the rock."

"You must have known what you were risking when you attacked Emmerson. He almost died," she said, her voice shaking.

"I thought I'd knock him out and he'd wake up a few minutes later with a cool story to tell. Like in the movies. I didn't realize how different it would be in real life. People are so fragile."

"People don't just bounce back up after they've been knocked out," she snapped. "Movies aren't real. Throwing rocks at people's heads can kill them, and Bigfoot doesn't exist!"

"I've devoted my entire life to this," Norman snapped. "I'm not crazy. Soon, even skeptics will have to believe in him"

"Is that why you attacked your friend?" she snapped back. "Because he was a skeptic?"

The gun wavered, and she gritted her teeth, watching him carefully.

"I thought if he survived an actual Bigfoot attack, he would start believing," Norman said.

"That's ridiculous, because he didn't survive an *actual* Bigfoot attack. He survived attempted murder. By you."

Norman seemed to think that if he could convince enough people Bigfoot was real, it would somehow make it true.

"You wouldn't understand. You only believe in what society tells you it's okay to believe in. People need to open their minds more. You're going to leave here with a very open mind." He raised the gun slightly, pointing it at her head now.

She ducked down as soon as she saw his finger twitch. Behind her, Samuel dropped into a crouch as well. He wrapped his arm around her waist, pulling her back and angling his body so he was between her and the gun. She didn't have time to argue. Instead, she just huddled against him, certain that at any moment they were going to hear a deafening gunshot and then, they would be dead.

But the sound never came. Finally, she peeked over Samuel's shoulder and saw Norman fumbling with the gun, the too-big costume gloves getting in his way.

"Stupid safety, I knew I should have turned it off before I put it in my pocket," he muttered. "And stupid gloves. Who designed these things?"

She didn't want to wait around until he managed to get the gun's safety off, but the only weapon she had was the pepper spray, and she still wasn't sure that was a good idea in such an enclosed space.

Then Samuel gently pushed her aside, leaving the knife on the floor beside her. Norman's eyes widened as he saw the other man approaching him, and he finally tore the glove of his costume off and reached again for the safety of the gun, but it was too late. Samuel shoved Norman in the chest, hard, and he went stumbling back. Tulia hadn't even realized he'd been standing on the top step up to the RV, and when the force of Samuel's push sent him back, his foot met only air, and he fell.

Tulia hurried forward, watching as Norman lay winded on the ground, his gun having vanished somewhere, probably knocked out of his hand by the fall. Samuel was quick on his feet and hopped down before Norman could get up, pinning the other man with a knee on his chest.

"I contacted the police while you were talking," he said, looking up at Tulia. He was breathing only a little bit hard, which she thought was unfair since her heart was thrumming in her chest like a humming-bird's. "They'll be here soon. See if you can find his gun. Without it, he can't do anything to us."

# EPILOGUE

When Tulia walked into the same diner she had met the cryptid hunting team in the week before, Melody was there waiting for her, her foot still in its ankle brace and a pair of crutches leaning against the wall next to the table.

Tulia joined her, a smile on her lips as she took in the half-finished plate of blueberry pie in front of the other woman.

"They say they have the best pie in the city."

"You know what, they just might be right," Melody said, taking another bite of it. "Thanks for meeting me. I wasn't sure if you'd still be in the area."

"It turns out, almost being murdered by a crazy

guy leads to a lot of questions from the police," Tulia said. "I'm heading out after this, but I wanted to see you first. How are you doing?"

Melody shrugged, poking her fork at the rest of her pie. "All right, I guess. Mason was … well, he was a really bad boyfriend. But seeing him die will always stick with me. I wish we hadn't gone camping that day."

"You couldn't have known what would happen."

"Yeah." The other woman gave a wry smile. "He made a joke about Bigfoot the day before we left. He was always a fan … not in the same way Norman was, and I don't think he actually believed it, but he probably would have laughed if someone told him a few years ago this was how he would end up going."

"How is your ankle?" Tulia asked, nodding at the clunky-looking boot.

"It hurts like the dickens sometimes, but everyone keeps telling me it'll get better. It already feels a lot better than it did last week, so that's something. I'm just glad you found me. I was certain I was going to die out there." She sniffed a little, and Tulia focused on the lump in her throat.

Samuel might disagree with her running towards a scream in the middle of the woods, and not away from it, but this was why she'd had to do it. Maybe all of her experiences during her trip should have made her more paranoid, but all they had really done was give her firsthand experience of what it felt like to be scared for her life, and she never wanted anyone else to feel that way. Not if she could help it.

"I'm glad I found you too," she said. "You'll keep in touch, right? If you're interested, I have a blog you could follow." She didn't share her blog with everyone she met, but Melody had definitely earned it.

"I'd like that."

Tulia scribbled out the name of the blog on a napkin and passed it over. "You might want to skip over the two most recent posts. I shared a lot of what happened to me out there. It might be upsetting for you."

"It might actually help to read things from your point of view," Melody said. "Oh, I called the hospital, but they couldn't tell me. Did that guy ever wake up? The one who was with Norman and that woman?"

"Emmerson? Yeah. Thea called me over the weekend. He's awake. He might even be out of the hospital by now. What happened the day you left? I never got the chance to ask you."

"The police came in to update me on the case and

revealed they were treating it as a homicide. Something about knowing they thought another person killed Mason, and not a wild animal, made me remember certain things about the attack that didn't fit, and I realized what I thought was Bigfoot was probably just a person in a costume. Then I thought about what a weird coincidence it was, surviving a fake Bigfoot attack and then running into three people who just happened to be hunting said Bigfoot, and I realized it must have been one of them. I was afraid if they visited me again, I'd let something slip, and they'd realize I knew. I didn't feel safe there anymore, so I left. I still don't get how he made the attack so convincing, though."

"He managed to get some weird concoction of oils from animal scent glands and drenched the suit in it," Tulia said, remembering what the police had found out when they questioned him. "The fur was a mix of moose and bear fur. The police think he might have had a taxidermist friend or something. And the prints came from custom 3D printed boot covers. He hid the whole setup in the woods a few minutes' walk from his camp."

Melody wrinkled her nose. "That's almost creepier than if Bigfoot really was out there somewhere. I think my camping days are over, for a long while at least."

Tulia grinned. "I've got to admit, I feel the same. I've had about enough of nature. For my next stop, the only trees I plan on seeing are potted ones."